To my great-granddaughters Charlotte Rebecca Burrows and Olivia Burrows
—S. I.

For Michael and Eira
—A. C. L.

Published by
PEACHTREE PUBLISHERS, LTD.
494 Armour Circle NE
Atlanta, Georgia 30324
www.peachtree-online.com

First published in Great Britain in 2000 by Bloomsbury Publishing Plc
38 Soho Square, London W1V 5DF

Designed by Dawn Apperley

Printed and bound in Hong Kong by South China Printing Co.

10 9 8 7 6 5 4 3 2 1
First Edition

ISBN 1-56145-223-8

Cataloging-in-Publication Data is available from the Library of Congress

Flora the Frog

Shirley Isherwood and Anna C. Leplar

PEACHTREE

ATLANTA

Flora's class was going to give a play about creatures who lived in the woods. All the children in the class were very excited. Miss Brown clapped her hands. "Quiet, everyone," she said.

"Now I will tell each of you which part you will have in the play. John, you will be a fox."

"I want to be an elephant," said John.

"There are no elephants in the woods," said Miss Brown firmly. "You will be a fox."

"Katie, you will be a squirrel." Katie smiled, for she liked squirrels.

"James, you will be a rabbit." James was pleased. He had two rabbits at home, so he knew just how they hopped and twitched their noses.

"But we must have some trees, too," said Miss Brown. "Who would like to be a tree?"

Some of the children raised their hands.

"Good!" said Miss Brown.

And then she turned
to Flora. "Flora," she said,
"you will be a frog."

Flora thought, *I don't want
to be a frog.* But she didn't
say anything.

When it was time to go home, she ran to the school gate.
Her mother and Aunt Jo were waiting for her.

"I'm in the class play," said Flora. "I'm a frog."

"How wonderful!" said her mother. "I was a fairy in my class play.
I had beautiful, gauzy wings."

"I was an elf in my class play," said Aunt Jo. "I had pointy shoes
with bells on the toes. I loved being an elf."

"I'll make you a special frog costume this weekend," said Flora's mother.

"I'll help you," said Aunt Jo.

"We'll make long, green legs," said Flora's mother.

"And a fat, green tummy," said Aunt Jo.

Flora wished that she could be a fairy with wings or an elf with bells on her toes.

The next Monday, the costume was ready. "Take it to school to show the children and Miss Brown," said Flora's mother. She folded the frog and put it in a bag.

As Flora hurried along with her mother, she saw that one of the frog's hands was hanging over the rim of the bag. It flipped up and down, as though it were waving to her. Flora poked it back inside the bag.

When Flora reached the playground, she saw that Maria, Katie, James, and John were together, practicing being the creatures in the play.

They're all something nice, thought Flora, *and I'm just a fat, green frog. I don't want to be a frog.*

She looked around, and when she thought that no one was looking, she took the frog costume from the bag and threw it up into a tree. It hung over a branch, with one of its hands sticking out from the leaves.

All morning, Flora looked through the window and saw the frog's hand. It swayed back and forth in the breeze, as though it were waving to her again.

In the afternoon, the children rehearsed their play. Everyone tried very hard to be good in their parts—except Flora.

"I don't want to do it," she said.

"But why, Flora?" asked her teacher. "I picked you to be the frog because you jump so well. You can jump higher than anyone else."

Flora didn't answer. She thought, *If I say that everyone is something nice, and I'm just a fat, green frog, then everyone will laugh at me.* She marched to her desk and sat down.

Glancing through the window, she saw that the hand had stopped waving. It was almost as if the frog knew what she was thinking.

"Did everyone like your frog costume?" asked Flora's mother that afternoon.

"Yes," said Flora. She finished her snack, took her ball, and went out to play. Her mother and Aunt Jo watched her. Flora knew they had guessed that something was wrong. She felt awful. She had thrown the frog costume into a tree, and she'd told a lie.

Why couldn't someone else have been a frog? she wondered angrily. She threw the ball so hard that it bounced over the fence and into the garden next door.

Flora sighed, then slipped through the gap in the fence.

She ran across the lawn to where her ball had come to rest
next to a small pond. Sitting on lily pads were three green frogs.
"*R-R-Ribbitt!*" they said, as though they were saying hello to her.

Flora knelt and gazed at the frogs. The frogs gazed back. They looked as if they were smiling. The sight made Flora smile, too. Then the frogs jumped, one after another. Up they went, with their long legs trailing, and each frog spangled with silvery drops of water from the pond.

Flora thought of the little bag of spangles in her mother's sewing
box. "I could have spangles on my frog costume!" she said to herself.
"How wonderful to be a spangled frog, jumping high in the air!"
Then she remembered.... "But my frog's in the tree!"

Flora ran back to her house. "He's in the tree! I thought
I could sew spangles on him, but he's in the tree!..."
Tears ran down her face, and she hiccuped.
"Spangles?" said Flora's mother.
"In a tree?" said Aunt Jo.
"My frog," said Flora. "I threw him into a tree."
She rubbed her wet cheeks and looked at her mother and aunt.
"Everyone else was something nice, and I was just a frog," she said.
"I didn't want to be one, but then I saw some real ones with spangles...."

"Frogs?" asked Flora's mother. "With spangles?"

Flora nodded. Tears began to roll down her cheeks once more.

"I know just how you feel," said Aunt Jo. "I didn't want to be an elf until the bells were sewn on my shoes."

"Blow!" said her mother, holding a tissue to Flora's nose.

"Come on," she said when Flora's face was dry. "Let's go and get him."

"I've come to take you home!"
said Flora, as she and her mother
and Aunt Jo ran into the school yard.
She jumped as high as she could,
grasped the frog's hand, and gave it
a tug. Down he came, with his long
arms falling over her shoulders, as
though he were giving her a hug.
    "Oh, frog...," she said. "I'll love
being a frog!"

Then all three hurried home to sew on his spangles.